Hand-lettered by the author

PUBLISHED BY BLOOMSBURY PUBLISHING, NEW YORK, LONDON & BERLIN DISTRIBUTED TO THE TRADE BY HOLTZBRINCK PUBLISHERS

LIBRARY OF CONGRESS CATALOGING-IN-PUBLICATION DATA AVAILABLE ON REQUEST LCCN: 2005040987

ISBN-10: 1-58234-672-0
ISBN-13: 978-1-58234-672-4

FIRST U.S. EDITION 2005 PRINTED IN CHINA 1 3 5 7 9 10 8 6 4 2

BLOOMSBURY CHILDREN'S PUBLISHING 175 FIFTH AVE NEW YORK NY 10010

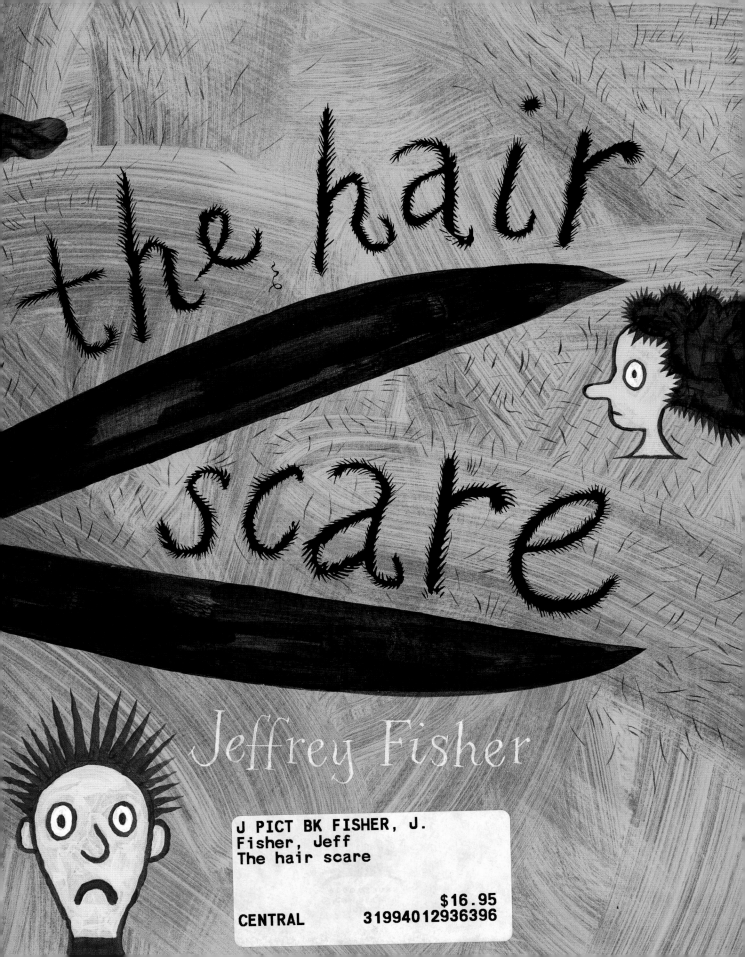

the hair scare

Jeffrey Fisher

Radbert liked
to cut,
and he liked
to cut
hair.

His mother, who had particularly attractive hair, fell asleep one afternoon.

Next in line was Father.

He was amazed and thought
Radbert was brilliant.
What would the
neighbors think?

They wanted haircuts of their own.

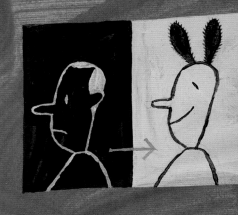

Radbert cut
and cut

and cut

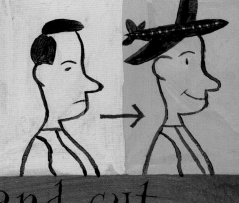

and cut.

Almost immediately, there was a
knock at the door; it was the King.
He wished the royal hair be cut
and he wished it be cut very nicely.
"Should you fail, there will be
trouble throughout the land",
muttered the King,
wriggling in his chair.

Radbert produced the best haircut in the history of best haircuts.

The King did not look happy.
He looked from the back,
the side, the front and the top.
An unpleasant silence
descended.

"This be the **WORST** haircut there be **EVER**", he spluttered.
"There be **NO MORE SCISSORS**. I command **AN END** to hairdressers."

There was trouble
throughout the land.
Locks hung heavy.
What would happen
now?

Nasty hair accidents, hair sadness and hair riots were on everyone's minds.

The King's hair grew so long, no one recognized him. He was soon forgotten. "WHO IS THAT MAN?" they asked.

There was a knock at the door.
It was the King. Again.
He wished the royal hair
be cut and commanded
it be cut very nicely.

"I'm afraid I no longer cut hair. My only interest now is in flourless chocolate cake," said Radbert.

"If my hair be not cut, I will **FORBID** ovens, sugar and all cocoa products," yelled the King. "And eggs..."

Radbert produced a better haircut than the best haircut in the history of better haircuts.

The King looked at his haircut. The haircut looked at the King.

In a great flutter
the King was lifted from
the floor

and flown directly
out of the window into
the night sky.

From then on,
the land returned
to Radbert's haircuts,
chocolate cake
and happiness.

And every now and then, the distant
grumbles of the King could be heard.........

"no lemons"......

no birds......

no ice cream......

no more onions......

no more kindness......